SHOT DOWN

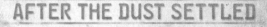

AFTER THE DUST SETTLED

SHOT DOWN

JONATHAN MARY-TODD

darby creek

MINNEAPOLIS

Darby Creek
A division of Lerner Publishing Group, Inc.
241 First Avenue North
Minneapolis, MN 55401 U.S.A.

Website address: www.lernerbooks.com

Cover and interior images: © iStockphoto.com/77DZIGN (cross hair target); © iStockphoto.com/Lou Oates (antique blank album page, background); © iStockphoto.com/Anagramm, (burnt edge, background); © iStockphoto.com/Evgeny Kuklev (aged notebook background); © iStockphoto.com/kizilkayaphotos (coffee stain); © iStockphoto.com/José Luis Gutiérrez (fingerprints); © iStockphoto.com/Bojan Stamenkovic (burnt paper background).

Main body text set in Janson Text LT Std 55 Roman 12/17.5.
Typeface provided by Adobe Systems.

Mary-Todd, Jonathan.
 Shot down / Jonathan Mary-Todd.
  p. cm. — (After the dust settled)
  Summary: When a bullet knocks Malik and the Captain's hot-air balloon out of the sky, landing them in the Kentucky wilderness, they are chased by man-hunters who believe hunting the weak is their post-apocalyptic duty.
  ISBN 978–0–7613–8329–1 (lib. bdg. : alk. paper)
  [1. Survival—Fiction. 2. Hunting—Fiction. 3. Kentucky—Fiction. 4. Science fiction.] I. Title.
PZ7.M36872Sh 2012
[Fic]—dc23   2012006864

Manufactured in the United States of America
1 – PP – 7/15/12

To my boyhood dog, Macbeth—
the events of this book
do not reflect the depths
of my affection

CHAPTER ONE

After something shot through the Captain's hot air balloon and we started sagging toward the ground below, I tried to remember the *Gene Matterhorn Wilderness Survival Guidebook* Path of Action in a Crisis. It came to me right before I hit the water. Or maybe right after. In a crisis, these things are hard to keep track of.

Step One: Scope Out the Scene.

I spat back the foamy water that had started to fill my mouth and looked around in every direction. High hills formed walls around us. Tree branches split off above me and reached out like veins across the sky. The river's current slid me forward 'til I grabbed a fallen log. *Rocks ahead*, I thought. *Hold on.*

Step Two: Take a Personal Health Check.

"Captain!" I shouted, the taste of river water fresh on my tongue.

My mind spun, and I rubbed a free hand along my shaved head. No cuts, no blood. I shouted for the Captain again. *It's crucial to determine your own well-being before attempting to help others*, the guide says. No noticeable wounds would have to be good enough.

I looked again and saw the Captain ten or twelve arm's lengths back. He was floating facedown in the water, half-hidden by his blue overcoat. I took my arms off the log and swam back his way, pushing against the current.

My arms burned by the time I dragged the Captain's huge frame onto shore. A small whine drifted out of his mouth—breath. I started pushing down on his chest, trying to remember as I went how many times the guide said to do it. The Captain didn't move.

I spat out more river water and lowered my mouth down onto his damp orange beard. Two breaths into his mouth—nothing. It wasn't 'til I started pumping his chest again that the Captain opened his eyes. He coughed up water, bubbling like a pot at boil, and then heaved forward, panting for air.

"Ack!" he said. "I just about bought the farm there, didn't I?"

"What?"

"Figure of speech—ah, never mind. I forget sometimes you grew up in the middle a' nowhere." He shook his head, his beard flinging water in all directions, and leaned back against a clump of grass. "Thanks for the, eh, life-savin', by the way."

Step Three: Inventory Your Remaining Resources

Together we walked up and down a stretch of riverbank, gathering what we could from the balloon crash. I reached into my pocket and pulled out a compass—cracked, the little arrow in the center bent. Useless.

A dozen steps away from where I'd lugged the Captain out of the river, I spotted a red-and-brown lump. My backpack. It had hit the ground when the balloon crashed, or maybe dropped out while the craft plummeted, but there was nothing inside that would've broke. Mostly clothes, a couple blankets, my worn copy of the Matterhorn guide.

The Captain shouted up ahead, "I found the food bags! The sack with the jerky got tore open, but you can look forward to dried leeks tonight, as per the usual." He started humming to himself and stuffing the stray snaps of jerky into his wet pants pockets.

The humming stopped as the Captain reached a clearing away from the riverbank. "Ah jeez," he murmured and dropped to his knees. "It's toast."

Inside a circle of ash trees, strung across twigs and dirt patches, were the ruins of his hot air balloon. The basket we had flown in— smashed. The reinforcements on the bottom were bent or in pieces. I stepped over a dented length of aluminum for a closer look.

The Captain looked up at me, pink-eyed. "I'm not sure there's any fixin' this," he said. "I can't even find my tools . . ."

A hiss grew louder and louder as I looped around the wreckage. Not like a snake's—steadier. I pushed back some shrubs with my foot and found the round white canister that had let us fly.

"Captain! The propane burner's over here."

"Well for goodness' sake, Malik, get away from there!" he shouted. He rose and moved to drag me away. "That thing could blow at any minute."

I took a few steps back. "Will it do that?"

The Captain heaved his soaked overcoat atop the burner. "Err. It might. You'd think it woulda already, if it was gonna, but then again . . . Gah! A thing like that's irreplaceable."

For a moment we stood and listened to the burner's muddled hiss.

"Should we duct tape it?" I asked.

"Yeah." The Captain nodded. "Let's duct tape it."

After I'd cautiously patched up any place where a leak might be, the Captain prepared to wrap up the burner in the balloon's envelope, the big tarp up top that fills with hot air. That was also too valuable to leave behind, the Captain said. He settled on tucking one inside the other.

As I was shoving the tape back in my bag, the Captain swore some curse I didn't recognize under his breath. He coughed for my attention and then stretched out a piece of the envelope in front of me. His hands shook: light shone through a circle-shaped tear.

"I didn't wanna call it 'til I knew for sure," he said, "but this's gotta be a bullet hole. Rifle fire, I'm guessin'."

Step Four: Make a Plan.

I took a long look at the hole. I asked why, like the guide suggested. Someone made a mistake, maybe, and fired a shot off on accident. Or, more likely, someone wanted to keep outsiders away. That was the story at a lot of places.

But for a plan? A real plan? I couldn't think of anything except hiding and hoping a better plan came to mind.

CHAPTER TWO

I met the Captain in a place called Des
Moines. It was north of the Kentucky hills
where we crashed, and colder too. I'd arrived
there while heading away from the Frontier.

The Frontier Motel was where I spent
my youngest years. Most of my clothes, my
blankets, I'd taken from there. Even *Gene
Matterhorn's Wilderness Survival Guidebook* had
spent years sitting in the motel common room.

My mother had stopped at the Frontier
before I was old enough to even read. I barely

remember the first year or two. They were the days when the world stopped working.

People were worried, my mother would say. She'd always mention how people's phones didn't work all the sudden. The motel was a place where people could stop and rest before they got where they were going. When everyone started to panic, my mom got off the road.

At the motel she got news of fighting in the east, bad storms all over. Some people headed back out, hoping to learn more. My mother stayed. Since I left the place, I've met different people who were sure of different things about what happened.

The Captain says he thinks it might've been aliens. But he also built his own hot air balloon in the middle of a city.

The Frontier was a safe place, away from whatever storms were out there. Nothing around it but trees and a gravel road. After a while, my mom and some of the other families that'd stopped decided to build a life there. I learned to hunt, learned to cook, and learned not to go very far. It wasn't 'til sickness hit the place, when I was fourteen, that everyone set out.

When I met the Captain in Des Moines, he'd seen some dark things too. He was living as a warrior and a mechanic, fighting off attacks, hunger, the cold. By the time he put his balloon together, I was ready to see the rest of the world. What was left of the world. We floated south, aiming to help people when we found them. Just looking for signs of life.

The Des Moines winter had turned into a gentle southern spring by the afternoon we got shot down. The Captain sat in the balloon's basket with his legs crossed, tying fruit along a string to dry out in the sun.

"So you never heard a' pretzel-style?" he said.

"What's that?" I asked.

"The way I'm sittin'. When I was a kid, I guess we called it Indian-style, but in yer adult life you realize that certain things like that tread on people's sen-suh-tivities," the Captain said. "Pretzel-style means yer legs are sorta shaped like a pretzel. It's a food."

"Growing up we ate deer and green beans. Then we ate more deer and green beans. I never had a pretzel."

The Captain pressed the wool hat he kept in his pocket against his sweaty brow. His grin showed rows of teeth like unripe corn. "Well, Malik, with sea salt and some nacho cheese, they are *dee*-licious."

He strung the fruit up with a tug and squinted into the horizon. "What I could really go for is some hash browns. I wonder sometimes if there's still a diner up and running somewhere. The Diner at the End of the World. No tellin' what kinda shape the southern hemisphere's in right now, but I tell ya, I'd trade this balloon some days for a hot cup of real coffee . . ."

I felt the wind change directions as I frowned at the Captain.

"This is one of those times we talked about," I said, "where you think we're having a two-person conversation, but I don't understand most of—"

The crackle we heard next could have been anything. To us up in the air, anyway. It could've been a tree falling or a thunderclap, I thought at first. But the sky was blue and the ground below was still. Above our heads, the balloon's patched-together envelope started to buzz like a swarm of wasps as air rushed out of it. And before I had time to wonder if we'd been right to jump from the basket, I was underwater.

CHAPTER THREE

We gathered up everything we could find from the crash, everything we could carry. Then we headed uphill. The Captain talked without stopping as we put more distance between us and the river.

"Looks sorta rocky up here, but all these trees'll keep us covered. Protect us." He stopped for a moment and eased his shoulders forward when the envelope holding the hissing burner started to slip down his back. "Coulda been an accident, of course . . ."

"The shot?" I asked.

"Yeah, the gunshot."

"But you don't believe that."

"Malik," the Captain said, "I *believe* we shouldn't take that chance. We lay low, as much as we can. These days, people tend to get defensive."

Defensive of what? I wondered. Most of what I saw around me was winding trees and green bushes, a few big chunks of rock rising out of the ground. But I'd grown up in a place that was hidden by woods. I tried not to trust everything I saw.

"You said it was a rifle that did it?" I said as the Captain leaned against a rock behind me. He'd been sweating hard since we'd started the climb.

"Yeah," he said. "Think so. Meeeaan weapon."

As we started to walk again, I kept thinking about who might've shot us down. *Why* they might've shot us down. I didn't know that much about what was out there in the world. Not really. That was part of why I'd said I'd travel with the Captain. Maybe they'd had a good reason, whoever did it. Though I couldn't believe they'd had trouble come from hot air balloons before.

I thought about the people I'd met since leaving home, too. I'd been attacked more than once: different people, different places. But of anyone I'd met whom I came to trust, who wanted more than to take something from other people—they never just attacked first. They wanted to trust people too.

The Captain got a rush of energy as the sun started getting lower, around the same time his coat dried out and started to stink. He shuffled between stones along a path made from the shade of broadleaf trees. I kept my head down, watched the ground, and followed his heavy footsteps 'til he stopped.

"Look there," he said. He pointed sideways to a long rock overhang. It lay like a small cliff over a short stretch of hillside. Beneath the overhang was flat patch of grass and dirt stretching a few body-lengths back into the face of the big hill.

"That's our campsite for the night," the Captain continued. "All the protection from the elements that a cave offers, without the risk of accidentally tripping over a sleeping bobcat."

We agreed to no fire for the night. Either the flame or the smoke could give us away to whomever might be looking. I told the Captain that in the morning I'd use the Matterhorn guide and go see if I could find any plants we could eat.

"Worse places to be shipwrecked than Kentucky," the Captain said as he started to fade. "Assumin' this is definitely Kentucky. There's probably no place around that still makes bourbon, but a man's gotta have dreams . . ."

• • •

I woke up sore in the morning. I couldn't get a sense of how long I'd slept for, but the sun was high. A few lengths away, the Captain was still out. He opened his eyes to a gun's thunderclap.

The sound wasn't near, but it burst out from someplace closer than when we'd been flying. I yanked up my backpack, and half the stuff inside dropped out the top: spare clothes, the duct tape. The Captain pulled together everything around him but didn't move his feet. We looked to each other, silent, and waited for another shot. Somewhere a dog howled.

Before the next gunshot came a weak hum of voices. No clear words—too far away—but it was people speaking. Another crack from a gun filled the air. The voices grew, but just barely. I stayed as still as I could and tried to figure out the how far they were away, what direction they were coming from. Then came the sound of running, louder from moment to moment. One person, rushing closer.

The Captain and I kept silent and stepped deeper under the overhang. Somewhere to my left, above us, I heard the runner's feet crush twigs and bushes until he fell with a grunt. A breath later, we saw a man begin to limp across the ground in front of us, underneath the edge of the overhang.

For a moment he stopped and stared. The man was middle-aged, with dark eyes and a cracked face. His beard was black with streaks of white, and black curls ringed the back of his head. He wore torn clothes, with one pale-blue shirtsleeve dangling under an armpit. Gasping for air, he took his hands off his bleeding shin and shook them, whipping his head from side to side.

I understood: stay quiet.

From down the runner's path I could start to make out voices:

"I think you dinged him, Dad!"

"Sssh! Pay attention now, Kyle! As long as he's alive, you stay on your guard. We've already let him out of our sight . . ."

Fear flashed through the panting man's eyes. One more time, he begged in silence for us to stay quiet. He didn't look like a danger to anybody. As the voices got closer, he took a last look at me and the Captain and then skipped off to my right, favoring his good leg.

The Captain and I stayed as far back as we could under the ceiling of the overhang, sticking to the wall of rock behind us. I closed my eyes and heard a final shot. A clipped but savage scream trailed over from the runner's path. And then a kid's voice, a boy's:

"Nice shot, Pop-Pop!"

A grown man's voice responded, warm and rich. "I think he's down now. I meant each word of what I told you, son. When I was your age, your grandfather taught me everything I know. And he can still shoot like the best of them!"

The men were close enough that I could hear the soft crunch of the bushes or branches they pushed out of their way. Three of them, maybe four. Somewhere above us, behind the overhang. The distances away steadied for a while—they were walking a straight line through the trees toward the body, not curving around the top of the overhang. They'd miss us, more than likely.

The man spoke up again.

"Kyle, I want you to wait here with your pop-pop. Past that ledge, the hill can get steep. You can hold the rifle if you like."

"But Dad, I wanna help you find the kill!"

"That's why we bring these guys, remember?" the man said. "This is when we release the hounds."

CHAPTER FOUR

The Captain gripped my shoulder. His paw of a hand twitched.

"Ah jeez, Malik," he said, "they're manhunters!"

A howl came over our heads from somewhere deeper in the hillside woods. The dogs were loose.

"Bloodhounds, I'd bet, or something like 'em. Trackers. Let's hope they stay on that other poor guy's scent."

"Do we run?" I whispered.

The Captain bit his lip and thought.

"I dunno," he said. "No. Even if the dogs miss us, we're close enough that those men might spot us. We stay."

The hounds scampered in the distance toward the running man's body. I heard light leaps, from maybe two of them, mostly in my left ear and then mostly in my right. The Captain rested the back of his head against the rock wall and sighed heavily.

Then the leaping stopped. Somewhere above the overhang, the dogs slowed to a walk. Quick, scattered steps sounded against the ground. I began to hear them wheeze and snort—sniffing out something new. From closer and closer to us.

"Dad!" the young boy called out. "Why did Maybelle stop?"

The older man hesitated before answering.

"She and Maggie might have caught a different scent." He paused again. "Kyle, you and Pop-Pop stay here."

At what sounded like the edge of the overhang, one of the hounds stopped, sniffed furiously, and let loose a long howl. One level below the dog, the Captain and I looked to each other. We traded uneasy nods. Then we ran.

We started downward, the rock overhang maybe keeping us out of sight 'til we were out of shooting range. I pulled my backpack onto my shoulders as I stumbled between rocks and logs. The Captain and I had needed the length of an afternoon to make it up the steep hillside. I wondered how long the dogs would continue to give chase.

With a patch of grass in front of me, I glanced back to see a second hound join the first atop the overhang. The two animals had mangy brown coats. They looked long and lean. They stared at me and the Captain and gave sharp barks, then skittered down either side of the overhang.

The more I ran, the harder it was to know how far the Captain and I had gone. I saw tree after tree after tree when I looked up, a blur of dirt patches and loose stones when I looked down. My soreness hadn't left, and my legs burned with each step. Another glance back showed the hounds rushing between trees— well below the overhang. Above them, on the rocky edge, was a small figure—the father of the boy?—staring down, standing stiffly. He had yellow hair and green and brown clothes. He didn't look to be following the dogs down. Just watching.

"Aagh! Huffff—"

A few lengths in front of me, the Captain had tripped across a stone that stuck out at an angle from the ground. He landed on his side and rolled forward, trying to regain his footing.

"Ah! Burner! The burner!" he said as the lump inside the balloon's envelope dragged along the ground, tied to the Captain's overcoat at his shoulder.

I grabbed his collar as I passed and yanked up, not stopping. My arm jerked straight and my feet kicked in the air as I lost the grass underneath them. My hip hit the ground first with a dull thud. The Captain righted himself and stuck out a hand.

"Not yer fault," he said. "We're in different weight classes."

Behind us, the hounds were getting larger. They wove through trees and bushes like they'd memorized a map.

The Captain started to jog ahead of me as I got my bearings. With one hand he held the wrapped-up burner at an arm's length, and with the other he waved in front of us. A narrow ledge jutted out in both directions, clinging along the hill from left to right as far as I could see.

"We find a way farther down, past that," the Captain huffed, "an' maybe the dogs can't follow..."

Or maybe we get trapped, I thought, running again. The ledge looked sixty strides away, maybe seventy. The dogs would reach it a few moments after we did. More sharp barks sounded throughout the trees.

I stepped out onto the short cliff a few breaths before the Captain.

"Where was this when we headed up?" I shouted.

"We musta climbed around it. We run along the edge for long enough and there's gotta be a path toward the river!"

The Captain waved for me to take lead, and I picked left. After twenty or thirty strides it sounded like the hounds had touched down on the ledge. I stole a look back and saw nothing, then turned in time to hit a fence. No—not a fence. A lean-to.

The sheet of sticks and leaves lay stretched across the narrow path. "Get behind this!" I told the Captain.

"Wha—?"

"It's a lean-to—a shelter. We weren't the only ones making camp."

We pushed the lean-to sideways on the path between the dogs and us and braced ourselves. And waited.

"You think the man we saw running was hiding out here too?" I asked.

"He looked like he mighta been out here for weeks," the Captain said. He looked up and down the lean-to. "Think this'll hold?"

"I wasn't sure your balloon would ever

leave the ground, but that worked."

He thought about that for a moment and shrugged. "Here they come."

The dogs bounded around the corner side by side. They didn't slow down as they approached the lean-to. I held tight to the long branch that ran across the top and closed my eyes.

I opened them again and hopped backward with both feet, keeping my arms stretched forward to hold the lean-to in place. A glance to my right showed the Captain had done the same. Both of the hounds snarled and bared their teeth. Their heads were stuck between different pairs of up-and-down poles. On the other side of the lean-to, the dogs tried to twist free, hind legs kicking up dirt and pebbles. One hound snapped its jaws in fury an arm's length from my waist.

The Captain looked to the bodiless heads of the trapped dogs and then to me.

"I'm about to propose somethin' I'm not very proud of, Malik."

"Propose it fast!" I yelled.

"It's a few steps to yer left before the big drop-off—"

The dog nearest the Captain wiggled its neck back, then drove its head forward again, toward his groin.

"—an' if we don't want these dogs on us in another minute, we gotta push in that direction."

Still gripping the lean-to's heavy crossbar, the Captain and I tugged toward the end of the ledge. The wood poles of the lean-to dragged the hounds along with it. Again I heard the dogs' legs scramble, pushing in the other direction.

At a foot's length away, I stared down the long drop-off. The height of ten men, maybe fifteen.

"Alright now," the Captain shouted. "Heave!"

The lean-to slid off the ledge, the dogs dangling with it in the air. And then— "Ack!"—the Captain fell to the ground and started to slide toward the ledge's rim too. The limp balloon envelope, burner inside, was tangled around a bar on the lean-to's frame.

Still tied to the Captain's shoulder, it dragged him forward.

"Your coat!" I shouted. "Take off your coat!"

Below my line of sight I heard one dog slip from between the lean-to bars and start the drop. It howled until it hit the next stretch of ground, crumpling.

I grabbed at the Captain's skidding feet, which carved crooked lines in the dirt as they moved along. He wriggled on the ground, wide-eyed and with arms stretched out, until the heavy coat slipped out from under him.

I fell backward against the ledge's rock wall in time to hear the second dog hit the ground below. And then a bursting—the burner blowing open. The treetops before me rattled, shaking off leaves.

The Captain peered over the ledge with caution. "Ah jeez," he whispered, panting, then went quiet. Any hope we'd had of flying away was destroyed in the drop beneath that ledge.

CHAPTER FIVE

The burning smell seemed to follow us in every direction. We stood stalled on the ledge after failing to pick a path out.

"You know what the worst part of this is?" the Captain said, pink-eyed again. "I'm a dog person."

"That's the worst part?"

"You know what I mean." He sighed. "I had a dog in Iowa, you know. For a while. A little Yorkie. His name was Petey."

"Those dogs were gonna kill us. Or hold

us 'til those . . . guys with guns came."

The Captain fanned himself with his cap, then used it to shake away a trail of rising smoke.

"I know that. Come on, kid. I know that. 'S not the point. Remorse is important. Keeps ya human." He tugged his hat back on and took it back off as the sun got higher and glared. "You practically grew up in the woods, Malik. You never had a pet?"

I shook my head.

"See? That's yer problem. Lotsa valuable lessons there."

I rolled my shoulders and tightened the straps on my bag. "You can tell me what kinds later. What are we going to do about the men out there? The manhunters."

"Unsentimental. Too unsentimental," the Captain murmured. His face turned serious. "The balloon's gone. That explosion got the burner, burned the envelope. They might've shot us down again anyways. Gah! You don't know how many nights I spent workin' . . ." He sighed again. "Anyways, that's a bust. Maybe unsentimental's the order of the day. What do you think? What'll that survival book a' yours recommend for putting together some mode of transport?"

"I can look through it. But—I mean, for now—do we hide? If they were still chasing, I think we would've heard them—"

The Captain squinted at me. "Do we hide or what, Malik? I'm not sure what yer gettin' at. We hide until we can get outta here. Or preferably get out of here, hide, and then go even farther, in that order. You heard what they did to that man who was running. We can't think even a camp deep in the hills is safe for that long."

"If there's no easy way out, though . . . don't you want to know what we're up against?"

The Captain got red in the face and forgot about keeping quiet. "These are men with *guns*, Malik! If we're lucky enough to figure out which way they went off to, we go the opposite direction, fast!"

"I can track them," I said. "If we get back up the hill, I know I can. Don't you want to know why they're killing people?"

"No!"

I looked up, deep into the mess of rocks and treetops. "We're lost. We got almost nothing. If we can know them—anything more about them—it could help us."

"Malik, I respect you. You know I do. I think you are a bright young man. But as the only adult here, I'm sorry, but I'm makin' an executive decision—"

But by then I had started up. The Captain scowled, folded his arms, and waited for me to turn around. When I didn't, he began to follow behind. I think the fear that sound would travel was the only thing that kept him from yelling curses at me.

At what felt like the start of afternoon, we neared the overhang where the hounds had sniffed us. Both of us moved forward an arm's length at a time. I climbed up a few rocks and raised my eyes even with the overhang, then above it. The short climb we had left to the top of the hillside looked open—no hunters in sight.

As I stepped past the overhang, further into the woods, a blinking light caught my eye. A red dot, on and off. I reached down and picked up a black disc. Small but heavy. The red light blinked from one corner. Around the disc's rim were *N* and *S* and *E* and *W*.

"I know what this is," I whispered to myself. "Captain! I found a compass."

He trudged up the hill behind me, past the overhang. I held the compass toward him.

"See? It's a good sign," I said.

"Terrific," he said, not looking at it, and walked past me, shaking his head.

CHAPTER SIX

At some point in the afternoon the long hill flattened out. The hunters had left a trail of broken twigs and bent plant stems most of the way to the top. What looked like maybe wheel tracks, too. I had spent the last stretch of our climb up paging through the Matterhorn guide.

I sat down on a rock and held out two handfuls of wild tubers to the Captain when he reached me.

"Thanks," he said, quiet, glancing from side to side. "Starved."

I took a lot of eating to feel full on foraged food. Sometimes more food than it was easy to find. But Kentucky seemed like anyplace else I'd been—a little bit of knowledge meant you wouldn't starve.

For a while we'll have to stick with plants, I thought. The Captain and I had hunted before. But with meat we would've ended up leaving traces of the kill or the prep or the meal behind—bones, blood, fur. That wasn't even thinking about starting a fire, or the smoke that comes from it.

The Captain wiped his mouth, and we kept walking. Not long after the ground flattened out we saw a building. Built from logs, boxy—not a house. A smooth gray walkway led up to one of its doors.

"'Nature Observatory,'" the Captain said, reading the yellow letters on a post nearby. "We must be in a public park or sumpthin'."

Soon after that we saw the start of a paved road.

"It's gotta lead out at some point," I said. "Maybe if we follow it, we'll get a sense of where the hunters came from. We won't have a trail to follow like in the woods, but it could work. The man I saw at the overhang—his clothes didn't look beat-up like the man running's. They could've come from a house, or—"

"Alright," the Captain said. "But let's walk *alongside* the roads. Between the trees. That'll give us *some* protection, anyway."

That wasn't an option for very long. The trees started to thin as we followed the road. The path led to another road running across it and stopped. We could turn right or left if we wanted to follow the blacktop for longer. I took out the compass and tried to see which direction matched up with the each turn, but the blinking dot seemed to stay in the same place.

On the other side of the road in front of us was a short fence. Wood, dotted with chipped white paint. I looked from left to right and walked over to it. The boards creaked as I leaned against them.

"Holy moley," the Captain said from behind me. "I guess this is horse country, huh."

Green fields rolled up and down on three sides of me, nothing like the woods we'd just left. The shaky fence we stood by went on for a long stretch, bordering the grass. As far as we could see, long fences boxed in other parts of the fields too. Near the horizon a horse appeared, then two of them.

"Wild. Gotta be," the Captain said, pointing to a gap in a large section of fence in the distance.

The horses had shining coats, both of them. They stopped and seemed to nod at each other, then took off toward different places.

"This whole area's full a' horse stables. Or used to be," the Captain continued. "People used to race 'em. Never really understood the appeal, myself. I was more into stuff that had a guy behind the wheel of sumpthin'. The occasional demolition derby, maybe, although that's really a different sort of—"

"This mean you're feeling better?" I asked.

"No," he huffed. "I still think this is the riskiest, dumbest thing we could do right now."

I looked across the green fields in front

of us as the sun took its first dips back downwards. No telling which way the hunters had gone or what they were heading to.

"I hope you got a plan movin' forward," the Captain said. "We get out there any farther and we're exposed. No shelter out there in the fields. You understand that?"

I nodded, then crouched down and squinted at the paved road. "They must've taken something away from here, but it didn't leave any tracks." They could have been miles away.

The Captain stared at me, arms folded. "So . . . ? Are we headed left, right, or aimlessly into some fields of bluegrass?"

I had no idea, but I thought saying so could only make things worse.

"We'll go left," I said, waving toward the stretch of road in that direction. "But if we don't find anything, we can double back into the woods before nightfall."

The back of my head started to ache as we walked. I realized I hadn't had any water since the day before. I could tell from the weight of my backpack that my thermos was empty, but

I unzipped the top of the pack anyway, sorting through spare shirts and the Matterhorn guide. Only a drop inside the steel container.

Not long after we started down the road, I heard the Captain breathe out deep and plunk to the ground. I turned to see him resting against a roadside fencepost.

"Don't look at me like that," he said, trying to smile but sounding worn-out. "I'm not as young as you, you know. Need more breaks."

So far that day I'd been running mostly on fear. Fear and the urge to know what might be out there. But looking at the Captain's large frame leaning on the fence, I felt something else: guilt. I started to say sorry for dragging him up the hill, that we should've tried to agree first. And then I saw it.

"Turning left might've been the wrong choice," I said, gazing past the Captain. What looked like a thin trail of smoke rose from somewhere far in the other direction. "Wait here."

I hopped over the nearest fence and dashed into the field behind it, toward the top of a tall slope between dips in the fields. Beneath the smoke trail was the rare, almost unreal-looking glow of a lit-up house.

I hurried back to the Captain.

"I think . . ." I gasped, "I spotted them."

He turned his head toward the source of the smoke. "Back that way?"

"Yeah."

He looked the way I felt. Scared, not sure of what was next.

"We'll probably be out of sight for a while longer. I bet we can walk until the point where we turned."

"An' then, lemme guess," the Captain said. "Hands and knees the rest of the way?"

I nodded. If we didn't want someone to see us coming up on the house, we were better off crawling. "Hands and knees."

"If they have more dogs, Malik, I'm gonna be very upset."

CHAPTER SEVEN

I dragged myself forward along the grass until I reached the fence that surrounded the glowing house's massive lawn. The fence was a bold red color, I could tell even in the dusk, and it looked newer than the others we'd seen, or at least more looked-after—no peeling paint. I scanned the yard slowly as the Captain finished his crawl behind me. The sunlight had nearly faded by the time we got there, and the glow from the house got brighter.

I couldn't remember ever seeing a house so big. It was like three homes end-to-end. On the side of yard opposite us there was another house, or maybe a stable. Had to be a stable. A wide wood carriage was parked near to it, with four tall wheels. A stone walkway stretched out from the front of the main house, twisting like a small river. The house was a bold red, same as the fence.

"No dogs," I whispered to the Captain. "No guards of any kind that I can see."

We slid between the slats of the fence, the Captain muffling his grunts as he went.

From the edge of the yard I could see different walls and corners through open windows. Inside were rugs, framed pictures, long candles on candlesticks. The place looked warm, calm, safe.

The Captain and I followed voices around a back corner of the house. As we edged along the back wall, it got easier to tell that one was a woman's. The voice dangled above our heads from out of a window, and we ducked down.

"Eat your mushrooms please, Kyle."

"No, thank you," said the boy we'd heard earlier.

"Carter, tell your son to eat his mushrooms," the woman said.

"Kyle, listen to your mother," said the man who'd been out with the boy.

"Your pop-pop ate all of his," the woman added.

"Hrrrnnhh"—an even older voice drifted through the window, grunting or mumbling words I couldn't make out.

A fork or a spoon scraped slowly across a plate. The father, Carter, raised his voice like he was speaking to everyone at once. "We had a sad day today. Maybelle and Maggie were good dogs. The finest dogs I've ever hunted with. More importantly, though, they were a part of this family. And what do we say about family, Kyle?"

"Family is the most important thing!" the boy said.

"Mm-hmm. And Kyle, if you find yourself feeling sad about Maybelle and Maggie—"

"It's okay to feel sad, dear," the woman added.

"—I want you to think about all the good hunts you had in those woods with them. All the fun. We have to focus on the good when life presents a challenge."

Someone tapped their glass with a piece of silverware. The oldest man, the pop-pop, grunted in agreement.

"The people who . . . hurt the dogs are still out there," the father continued. The Captain and I looked to each other. He tilted his head away from the house—*Let's go*—and I shook mine no.

"We have to be strong for the hunt," the father said. "And why do we hunt?"

For a moment no one inside spoke.

"Kyle?" Carter asked.

"Because . . . um . . . it's our right, as those who survived!" the boy said. "Because it's something you earn, and, uh, the weak—the weak *get* hunted. So if you don't wanna be weak, you have to hunt."

"Very good," the father said. "The world is only fit for the strong now, Kyle. When I was your age, just nine or ten, your pop-pop said to me—Kyle, what do you have under the table?"

"Put that away, dear," the mother said.

"I don't have anything," the boy said quietly.

"Give it here, Kyle," the father said. Something clunked onto the table and started to roll. "A tracker? Son, what did we say about this? You already lost one today—"

"But Dad, it's blinking really fast!" Kyle cried out. "I bet I can find the other one—it's close!"

"Blinking?" the father said.

"Blinking?" the mother repeated.

The old man grunted harshly.

I patted my back pocket, feeling for the black disc I'd picked up earlier. Its red dot was blinking faster too.

"That's not a compass," the Captain mouthed.

We started off away from the house, running as fast as we could without making much noise. The sounds of the family scrambling away from the dinner table followed us from inside.

Nearer to the back fence I started a full sprint. Outside the family's front door, the young boy shouted, "There they are! There!"

I looked back for the Captain, who shuffled his feet a few steps behind me and cursed. When I turned back around, a black blur dashed across my path. A man on horseback—not one of the family. He pulled the horse to a halt in front of us, yelling for me and the Captain to stop right there. He held tight to a pair of reins in each hand—one for each of the horse's two heads. The animal stomped its front feet before me and the Captain, snorting fiercely from four nostrils.

CHAPTER EIGHT

I stared up at the two-headed horse, not believing. The man behind the reins said nothing. His hair was black and cut close. I couldn't make out his eyes in the darkness.

"Hold them there, Dennis!" shouted the father, Carter. I turned my head slowly to see him walking toward the edge of the yard, his rifle pointed at me or the Captain.

"Hands up," he said. "Don't move."

"I won't say I told ya so," murmured the Captain.

Kyle followed his father at a distance. The father kept his gun raised when he reached us. He looked up at the man on horseback.

"Thank you, Dennis. I think we'll be all right for the moment. Why don't you lead Roman back inside?"

The man on horseback, Dennis, nodded and then tapped the side of the horse with his boot. They took off around the edge of the house.

"You saw that, right?" the Captain whispered. "With the two heads?"

I gave a quick nod, trying to keep still for the man with the gun.

"We saw you earlier. You're responsible for the dogs," the father said. "What are you doing here?"

When neither of us spoke, he moved the rifle closer to the Captain's face.

"Close range," the man continued coolly. "Even with two of you, you try anything and you're likely to lose your head. Now—what are you doing here?"

"You, eh, shot us down," the Captain said. "Remember?"

The man's expression broke for a moment, flushed with anger. "This is my home. This is still very upsetting." He called to his son, keeping his stare on us. "Kyle! Come over here. Don't be afraid. I want you to reach into my back pocket—the ropes are there."

The boy edged forward and took the ropes, then carefully tied my wrists and the Captain's. With the extra rope hanging off, he tied our separate bindings together.

"Come on," the father said. "Slowly. We're going inside."

• • •

The hallways within the house were long and wide, lit on both sides by rows of candles. The floors below our feet were smooth wood, with rugs spaced evenly along them.

The son walked several steps in front of us. His father walked behind, still armed but with the gun at his side. Kyle led us into the room where they'd been having dinner.

The boy's mother looked frightened when we entered, but she forced a smile. "My wife, Georgine," the father told us. "Sit down."

The Captain and I took the two extra chairs Georgine had set out, our bound hands in front of us.

"We'd like to offer you dessert," the father said.

"The berries come from just outside," said his wife, nervous, still smiling. She lifted the top from a small round jar in the corner.

"I bet that's real refreshing after a big plate of people," snarled the Captain.

Georgine's face went sour, and she focused on the fruit, making a series of scoops onto shiny little plates.

"We only hunt," Carter said, "for *sport*."

A grunt trailed in from the hallway, followed by the squeak of wheels. The old man entered, the one we'd only heard before.

"We got 'em, Pop-Pop," said the young boy, speaking softly, like it was a secret.

I stared around the room from end to end. The grandfather in the wheelchair glared back at me while he parked at the table. His head was shaped like a brick, a flat face and a stiff chin. A few strands of white hair floated on top his head.

The father's jaw was square like the old man's, but ripples of blond hair topped his head. The young boy's face was rounder, like he hadn't grown into his family bones. The skin on both of them was a painful pink from too much sun.

The mother had a thin face, long cheeks, and hair that was browner than the others'. A blue-and-white-dotted apron hung around her neck. She began to put plates of berries around the table.

The Captain twitched in his seat, trying with each hand to scratch an itch underneath the bonds wrapped around the other hand. He seemed nearly finished with caution.

Georgine began to set forks in front of me and the Captain, then shook her head and went back to a drawer against the wall.

"You do dessert with most people you've tied up an' sicced dogs on, or are we sumpthin' special?" the Captain asked.

Anger flashed on Carter's face again. "We're trying to let you spend tonight with your dignity preserved. As much as we can. Don't throw it away."

"Sorry," Georgine said, setting down spoons where the forks had been. "Noooo sharp objects."

"Yep, this is real dignified," said the Captain.

I squinted at Carter, trying to make out what he'd meant. He seemed to pick up on it. He walked over to the pop-pop and set a hand on the old man's shoulder.

"My father taught me that composure, a sense of honor, self-respect . . . these are things by which we distinguish ourselves. What separate us from our lessers." He looked to Kyle, and the boy nodded in agreement.

"Those things, and power. The apocalypse, the Fall, the meltdown, the end of things . . . whatever you want to call what happened to this country. I've always believed it was an opportunity—the ultimate in social Darwinism. The chance for those of us who deserved it to really rise above. To continue what the end of things started—to claim our place in the world."

He took a few steps closer to me and the Captain.

"Now, as I said, we do it honorably. That's what tomorrow's all about."

The Captain turned his head toward mine. "I know yer not very worldly, Malik, so lemme translate: this is a crazy person."

The man kicked over the Captain's chair, and the dessert plates rattled from the crash. Kyle and Georgine set down their silverware and stopped chewing until Carter nodded that it was all right. He took a seat himself.

"You'll spend tonight in the stables. Tomorrow morning at sunrise you'll have one hour to make your way from the house. Then we'll start the hunt."

CHAPTER NINE

Carter walked us to the stable at gunpoint. His son trailed behind him, wheeling the old man.

"Maybe you'll meet Dennis, if he hasn't gone to bed," said Carter, sounding bored. "Later in the season we'll usually find some migrants to fish for us and mind the vegetable gardens, but Dennis stays here all year round, tending to the horses."

"Five whole people. The rulers of practically nothing," the Captain grumbled.

Kyle skipped ahead to open the stable's large wooden gate, then wheeled his pop-pop inside. The air in the place felt thick, and it smelled like hay and horse dumps. Four pens lined each side, but only three horses filled them. One was the two-headed thing we'd seen outside.

Carter led us to a pole in the center of the stable floor. It stretched up to the ceiling, touching the beams under the roof. A candle stuck out from a small ledge at about twice my height, the only light in the room. It made Carter's pink skin look pinker. He placed his gun in the lap of the old man.

"Kyle," he said, turning to the boy. "You can help me right now by running around back and getting a stick or an old broom."

The boy nodded and ran off. As he did, the man we'd seen on the horse—Dennis—entered the barn.

"Dennis! You'll have some charges for the night," Carter called over to him.

The man set down what looked like bags of feed by the entrance. He spoke in a low voice as he approached us. "Down to the last sacks. You know if the traders are coming soon?"

"We can only hope," Carter said.

When Kyle came back with a broom, his father snapped it in two under his foot. One piece longer than the other. After a few moments I understood why.

The old man held his rifle on the Captain as the father untied the Captain's wrists, then tied them back up behind the center pole. Each wrist was knotted to a different end of the piece of broomstick. Then they did they same for me, with the shorter part of the broken stick. The two of us sat bound to the same pole, but our hands were too far apart to untie one another's ropes.

My eyes met the old man's and he grinned, proud and yellow-toothed.

"If we get a trouble-free report from Dennis, we'll serve you some breakfast before we release you for the hunt," the father said as he, the boy, and the old man left the stable.

"Ah, thanks!" shouted the Captain. "I'll have the Denver omelet!"

"I admire your spirit!" Carter replied from out in the yard.

• • •

Dennis the stable-keeper walked between the horses' pens, leaving food someplace behind each metal gate. The two-headed horse chomped away with both mouths.

"What—" I started, seeing if Dennis would turn around to me. "What is it?"

"A mutation," he said slowly. He said everything slowly, low and flat. "That's what we think. It's more and more common, if you watch the fields, the woods. Don't know why. But this is the biggest animal we've seen to get so . . . different. Roman's special."

I looked up at him, waiting for more, but he had finished. After feeding the last horse, Dennis pointed above our heads, to the stable's one candle. "On or off?" he asked.

"I was thinkin' about a little light reading . . . do you wanna consult the horses?" the Captain said.

Dennis frowned and started to climb the wide wooden slats that took him to a bunk or a cot.

The ground in the stable was damp. I could feel the wetness seep into my pants, and I wondered where my pack was. Everything the Captain and I had left was in the family's house. Spare clothes, our cooking pan, the Matterhorn survival guide.

I thought again about the Path of Action in a Crisis. Step One: Scope Out the Scene.

Dennis was asleep—maybe. Through the stable entrance I saw the sky was black. We'd have the cover of night, at least, if we got loose.

Step Two: Take a Personal Health Check.

I was sore, but they hadn't hurt me. The Captain breathed heavily—he'd never sounded so tired—but when I asked he said he felt okay.

Step Three: Inventory Your Remaining Resources

In a stable, in any place near a house that big, there had to be stuff we could use. I pulled against the piece of broom on the opposite side of the pole, the ropes tearing on my wrists. A drop of wax landed on my head.

Step Four: Make a Plan

I turned to the Captain and whispered, "I need you to hold still for a few breaths. Then, when I say so, you stand. I'm gonna sit on your shoulders."

"What?"

Standing up on my side of the pole, I swung one leg toward the Captain's side and over his head, so I was stacked on top of him. Seated on his shoulders, I whispered for him to get up.

"Gonna blow my knees out," the Captain murmured.

Once he was standing, I started to stand too, leaning against the pole for balance and keeping one foot on each side of the Captain's neck.

The Captain's breathing got faster underneath me, and through my feet I felt him shaking slightly. No sound came from Dennis's bunk. Looking over my shoulder, I tried to spot the candle behind my back. Carefully, I began moving my bound arms toward the ceiling, trying to put the piece of broom that bound them in the candle's flame or right above it.

After a few nervous breaths, I started to smell smoke. One of the horses grunted below. "Almost there," I whispered down to the Captain.

As the wood began to crackle, I forced my arms forward and heard the stick snap behind me. The thrust sent me forward. I wheeled my hands back the other way, taking a foot off the Captain's shoulders and wrapping myself around the pole. One foot after another, I worked my way down, then undid the Captain's bonds.

"I'm impressed," he whispered. He took a step toward the yard outside, and I turned to the two-headed horse, not following.

"You got ridin' experience, Malik?" the Captain asked. I shook my head.

"Then now's prob'ly not the best time to learn. Let's get outta here before that guy smells the smoke an' wakes up."

The air outside the stable was cool, and the lights were out inside the house. I tugged at the Captain's shoulder, then tilted my head toward the house. "Our stuff," I whispered. "Do we risk it?"

"Absolutely not!" he hissed. "This time you are over*ruled*."

"That shed, then," I said, pointing to four tiny walls behind the house on the yard's far side. "We check it, then head out."

The Captain nodded his head and raised a finger to his mouth—*Be quiet*—in case I hadn't already known to.

We made an arc around the back corner of the house, stepping toward the shed. It felt like the longest walk I ever took—slow, silent steps, looking up to check the house's windows after each one.

The inside of the shed was dark, and its door faced away from the moon. I moved my hands along the wall, feeling for tools, 'til I felt the prick of a saw's tooth. I plucked the saw from the wall while the Captain grabbed a box of matches and a bundle of wire and then stepped back outside.

The Captain and I edged around the rim of the backyard, aiming to run for the long roads and then the woods, once we'd made it beyond the front lawn. We'd made it to the far side of the house when a glow caught my eye from a side window. I stopped for a breath and squinted in—and met the eyes of the woman, Georgine. She wore a heavy-looking bathrobe and carried a candleholder.

I waited another breath for her to scream. When she didn't, I made the same dumb be-quiet motion that the Captain had just made, pleading. Her face was blank, very still. She set down the candle and left the window for a moment. She showed up again a moment later, holding an archer's bow. The *thwip* of the bowstring cut through the air, and an arrow knocked the matches from the Captain's hand. He and I stumbled into each other, shouting out, as the awakening horses moaned from over in the stable.

CHAPTER TEN

It was foolish to go back the way we came, maybe. We knew that Carter and his family knew those woods. But in the other directions the rolling fields went on for as far as we could see. No telling how long we'd be in sight for—or from how far away one of them could pick us off. In the woods we were covered, at least.

The Captain and I didn't stop 'til nearly dawn, except for a few nervous moments to catch our breaths. Stayed on our feet. We

reached the river before the sun came up—
that or some stream that ran into the bigger
river or out of it. The water's flow was wide,
and the current seemed strong.

The Captain hunched over his shaky
knees, a ring of sweat around his neck.

"That saw ya took," he said. "Can we put it
to use? You know how to build a raft?"

"Huh?"

"Like a log raft, I mean. There wasn't
sumpthin' in yer guidebook about it?"

"I think so, probably, but I never had any
reason to try it. Do you know how to build
a raft?"

The Captain shook his head. "Nah."

"You built a *hot air balloon*."

"That's different! The balloon has fuel, and
controls, a tarp . . . a balloon is not a raft, Malik."

"Everyone in Iowa called you *the Captain*."

"Why did you bring a saw if you weren't
thinking of making a raft?"

"It was the first thing I grabbed!" I said. I
pictured the roll of duct tape inside my bag,
inside the family's house. "That coil of wire

you took—maybe we could start by tying some logs together."

We agreed to switch on and off. Whoever wasn't sawing at low branches was trying to bind the wood together. My hands began to tighten up after sawing off the first few logs. I yanked the saw back and forth, but more and more slowly, even when I tried to keep the same speed. Water. That's what I'd been missing. I tried to remember the last time I'd had a drink.

Once the Captain and I swapped tasks, I stepped over to the large stream. A long fish glided through the water, shining green-black scales, with one eye mounted above its mouth. Another fish glided behind it, the same.

I wondered if it was a trick of light, like something the guide had mentioned—how fish in the water are always in a slightly different place from where you think you see them. I must have been wide-eyed when I turned to the Captain, because he nodded his head.

"Yeah," he said. "You're not seein' things. Might be one of those mutations that guy in the barn was talkin' about."

"There aren't fish like that?"

"Not supposed to be. Not cyclops fish. Back when you were prob'ly just a little kid, there was talk of nukes goin' off . . . there was *already* junk in the air, in the rivers. But yeah, 's not natural. Maybe stay away from drinkin' the water a little longer if you can. We'll boil some, sometime soon. Might be a *little* safer, anyway."

He took the saw, moved toward a branch, and started speaking more to himself: "Be some kind of justice if that family started sproutin' tentacles a generation down the line . . ."

A glare fell on the water as the morning stretched out. I turned away and tried to bind the logs together, remembering wrong a bunch of knots I'd learned from *Matterhorn* and starting over a couple of times. So far we had a row of five logs tied up—enough for me to sit on pretzel-style, but not enough to carry me and the Captain. Taking a length of wire, I tried to line a sixth log up against the rest, forming a loop with the wire, forming another one, putting the end of that through the first loop . . . My mouth was dry and I couldn't swallow, and I looked back toward the water.

"Hey, Captain. Do we know where the river goes? Which way out of here?"

"No," he said. "Sun's up from the east, which I guess is over there, water's movin' the opposite direction . . . if it keeps goin' that way, no major kinks or turns, after a while we'd end up in, jeez, maybe Indiana? Ohio, if it veers north? The-places-formerly-known-as."

"But we don't know if it goes that far. Or even out of these woods."

The Captain set down his saw and frowned. "I suppose it could be emptying out into a lake or sumpthin'. I'll go follow it along for a while, check it out. In the meantime, you wanna act like you know we've been doin' sumpthin' smart? Saw some more logs if you run out?"

I nodded.

The noise by the water grew louder once the Captain left. The stream hissed along the rocks, and birds shook up ash-tree leaves. My own breathing sounded pained and uneven once I started to pay attention to it. With the Captain's logs, the raft was a body's-length long, but the whole thing creaked and curved near the center when I tried to move it closer to the water. Where was the saw? Maybe the raft needed logs underneath the logs, some supports.

I got to another tree with low branches, but I was sitting down there before I realized it. The shade hung over the ground where I lay, and my eyes went shut. Too hot. My hands hurt. My neck hurt. I had let go of the saw, and I picked it up again but my legs felt weak.

I don't know much of the morning passed before I opened my eyes again. A gun's thunderclap brought my head forward, and I looked to see bird feathers falling to the ground a few lengths in front of me, dropping one at a time into the stream.

"Warning shot!" a voice called out, echoing off the steep hillside from somewhere high above. "The hunt is on!"

CHAPTER ELEVEN

I was running again. I couldn't see anyone
from the family up above and didn't look
for long. I rushed off, away from the raft,
away from where the Captain had wandered
to. If they got me, they wouldn't get him too
without working for it. When I glanced back
at the raft every few strides, it didn't seem to
get farther away. I jerked my legs forward, step
after step, but the ground's pull got stronger.

They could probably see everything. I
touched the back of my neck as I ran, where

I imagined their eyes falling, like my hand would stop the bullet.

After hustling between trees for a while, I noticed a narrowing of the stream nearby. I took a few steps across the shallow water over to the stream's other side. The trees were thicker, and I started to double back toward the raft.

I couldn't even see the top of the steep hill where the shot had come from through the leaves and branches above my head. Either the family had moved on, looking for another way toward the river, or they had started down, hidden. But I was hidden too. I wiped my wet shoes into the dirt beneath me, slapped some mud across my shirt, and then pressed two fistfuls of leaves onto the mud. I could wait until they gave up, I thought. Or until I passed out.

I began to walk in a small circle around a cluster of trees, checking for movement in each direction and trying not to cramp up.

If I died it would be like disappearing. No one would bury me. No one would even know—maybe the Captain, if he stayed alive. I wondered if Carter or his wife kept a record somehow. A wall with shoes or scraps of clothing hung up, or a row of marks on a pole.

When the sun rose high enough to mark the end of morning, I began to hear someone crying out. Faraway shouts from across the stream. It was the boy, Kyle.

I stepped quietly closer to the water and peered forward. The boy lay several body-lengths back from the other side of the riverbank. One leg stuck forward, one leg was bent back. Behind him was a steep incline covered in mud and rock. His shouts grew louder: "Help! Dad, Pop-Pop, help! I fell!"

The boy was red-faced, and he didn't move from his spot on the ground. Maybe he couldn't. Every few breaths he started again: "Da-aad! Help me! I'm hurt!"

This was a trap. The boy's father was in a tree nearby, maybe, with a rifle pointed at the ground. Or somewhere on a ledge, the grandfather would pull back a stick that held a rock in place and it'd come falling on my head.

It was a trap—unless it wasn't. I looked at the squirming boy and shook off some of the leaves on my shirt.

It was several dozen steps to Kyle, not even counting the stream between me and him. If there were guns ready, I might know before I even reached him.

• • •

The boy was resting up against his backpack when I got close. His right leg was still bent behind him, but there were no rips in his pants, no blood. His face lost its color when he saw me, but I couldn't read it. He was afraid, or embarrassed. Or guilty.

For a few breaths, neither of us spoke.

"Where are you hurt, kid?" I said.

He pointed with a shaky hand to where his right leg was bent. When I took another step forward, he moved the hand to his mouth and let loose a broken whistle. He stayed silent once he'd finished, his face getting whiter still.

CHAPTER TWELVE

I lingered for a moment, too tired to sprint off. His father must have been far enough away that I didn't hear the gallops until a few breaths after the boy whistled. Even then they were quiet. Kyle must not have expected me to stay even that long—I wouldn't have either— and he met my glare with fear, confusion.

"I—I didn't think you'd try to help," he said. "That's never worked before."

"There's different kinds of strong," I said. "Putting people before yourself—that's one your dad didn't tell you about."

I rose up to run, and the boy held out a canteen, his hand still shaking. The body was hard, part metal. A heavy thing. Water sloshed around inside. I hung its strap around my neck and started back toward the stream.

"If this is poisoned," I called back, "you got me twice."

The sound of horse hooves got louder as I crossed the water again. Carter was heading to the spot where Kyle had whistled—that must have been how they planned it. I wove through trees, gulping water as I went. In the blur to my left, I glimpsed the boy's father riding the other way.

After the gallops disappeared, I thought I heard a rustling somewhere closer, in front of me. I slowed my run, then stopped completely.

"Captain?" I whispered.

"Malik!" He stepped out from behind the tree. "Thank goodness! They haven't caught you, huh?"

"No, but they're out there."

The Captain nodded. "I heard the shot."

"I got lucky," I said. "The man's headed the other way. Thinks he found one of us, but he might've already turned around."

"What about the raft? Far as I can tell, the river just keeps going."

"Good for a solid one and a half passengers? Our only way out of here."

"Alright then, let's go," the Captain said. We both started back in the direction I'd been running, the Captain shuffling behind me.

"You don't have the usual spring in yer step, Malik. You look tired," he said.

"You too." I tossed him the canteen. "Take a drink. It's a gift from the little kid."

"What?"

• • •

The woods around us were still—not even a strong breeze. The raft lay where we had left it near the bank. The Captain nudged it with one foot.

"It's gonna be wobbly," he said. "But maybe it'll be enough to get us headed outta here." He smelled his tattered T-shirt under one armpit. "Once we've put some distance between us and the wackos, first thing we do is find a way to get some changes of clothes."

I took a step toward the raft and glanced a yellow feather in front of my feet. The family had been close enough for one of them to pick off a bird above my head, I thought. Why did they leave the raft where it was, intact?

"Malik? We ready to depart?"

"Wait," I said, taking a sip from the canteen around my neck. "There."

A small red light flashed off and on in the shadow of a tree we'd cut logs from. One of the trackers.

"They hoped we'd come back here, if we'd joined up again! So they'd know where to find us—the tracker would lead them back!" I leapt over to the tree, reaching for the blinking light. "I'm gonna take the tracker, throw it up above, and try and lead them off cou—"

Something wrapped tight around my left ankle, brushing like a ring of fire against my skin and dragging my feet off the ground. My spine smacked against the knotted trunk of a tree, and the top of my head brushed the grass below. I was upside down, hanging by a thick rope.

"They booby-trapped it!" the Captain said. "Hold on, I'll getcha down! Un-freakin'-believable . . ."

"Careful!" My head spun and I tried to hurl myself upwards, toward the knot by my ankle, but I flipped back down. As the Captain moved to grab the rope, a shrill whistle pierced the air. The Captain stepped back out from underneath the shade of the tree and looked up.

"Ah jeez—up in the hills—the old guy's made us!"

"What?" I said, still spinning.

"The grandpa, the one in the chair! He's up on the hillside with a pair of binoculars—"

The whistle sounded again, and I shut my eyes 'til it stopped.

The Captain shouted upward, "Thank you! We get it!" and started scanning the ground for the saw we'd stolen.

"A-ha!" He waved it in the air and turned to face a path where the clopping of horse hooves had started to rise. "The saw will hafta do. Come on, you over-tanned psychos! We're right here!"

"Captain!" I said. "Could you cut me down before they get here?"

"I'm embarrassed to say that didn't occur to me," the Captain replied, then shouted one more time toward the pathway: "Do yer worst!"

Before he put the saw to the rope around my foot, they were on us. I saw them charging from upside down: the young boy, Kyle, on a small brown horse. And his father, Carter, riding the double-headed Roman, his rifle cradled in his free hand.

CHAPTER THIRTEEN

The father's face was calm, but his eyes seemed to sparkle. Or at least that's how it looked from upside down. When he spoke, after he'd steadied his horse, his voice sounded warm, controlled: "Put this back in your saddlebag, son," he said, and tossed Kyle the other tracking disc. The boy did as he was told.

Carter spoke to the Captain with the same sunny confidence. "I said it before: I admire your spirit, you two! For the amount of time, that little boat you've made over there is impressive."

As he spoke, I tightened up my stomach, moving my hands slowly up the back of my left leg, toward the knot at my ankle.

The Captain spat, and Carter pointed the gun toward his chest.

"This was a good hunt!" Carter continued. "Not our longest hunt, right Kyle? But this is a hunt we'll remember. We're going to have to . . . let Dennis go, unfortunately, for allowing you two to escape. Again, though, evidence of your ingenuity! It's a rare thing. Now, if either of you would like to say a prayer, any kind of last words, go ahead." He said to the boy, more quietly, "And why, again, do we hunt, son?"

The boy gripped the strap of his saddlebag and said nothing.

"Kyle?"

"B-because the world's only fit for the strong now," he said. He kept his head turned away from me.

"Aw, fer cryin' out loud, you creep," the Captain said. "Why not just admit to the boy that you *enjoy* it?"

The father's face went flat. "For that," he told the Captain, "we'll change the order up. You get to watch your young friend die first."

I couldn't see the Captain's face during what happened next. The end of Carter's rifle shifted my way, and the Captain said nothing more. He just stomped in between me and the gun and charged.

I shut my eyes and prepared to hear the Captain cry out. Instead I heard a *whulp!* and saw him slide under the front legs of Roman the horse. Roman neighed in alarm and jumped up, both heads confused. Carter was thrown off the animal's back. I saw him hit the ground with a thud. His rifle landed on its butt and fired off into the trees.

I jerked my head left and saw, right side up, the Captain scrambling. He'd stepped into another booby trap.

The gunfire scared Roman even more than the snagging of the Captain, and the horse ran off into the trees. Kyle struggled off the smaller horse—his animal had also started to panic, and it sprang away before Kyle touched the ground.

In the tree next to mine, the Captain grunted and hacked away at his rope with the saw still in his hand. I scanned the ground for Carter, who rose up in the cloud of dust the horses had left.

"Come back here!" he shouted, but they were gone. He scanned the ground himself until he spotted the rifle.

"Kyle!" the father said. "In the bag—I need bullets, now!"

By that time the Captain had plopped from the tree. He pounced and broke Carter's uneasy grip on the gun. The two men tumbled past the raft into low water. The young boy looked on, nearly still. One of his hands dug through the saddlebag.

I picked at my knot, the metal canteen swinging back and forth from the strap around my neck. Hanging there sideways, I saw the Captain tackle Carter, holding him in the water until Carter kicked loose.

The men moved back and forth, kicking up a spray of water in every direction. The father had to be younger by years, and he was leaner, too, but the Captain seemed to absorb the man's blows, pressing his weight. Before he sank the father's head under again, Carter cried out, "Kyle! The gun!"

When the Captain lifted him back out after dunking him under, Carter sank an elbow into the Captain's groin and the Captain went big-eyed, gasping. Water dripped from his beard while he stumbled backward.

"Now, Kyle!" Carter shouted, tightening one arm around the Captain's neck.

The Captain moaned and let his body drop back, thrusting Carter headfirst into the stream.

The boy pulled a round from his bag and skittered toward the rifle, glancing with each step at his father.

Blood swirled around in my head as I set my feet back on the ground and leaned against the tree. For a moment both men in the water rested a length apart on their hands and knees. Fighting for air.

Kyle kept his back to me and held the men in his sight. He might have been spooked, but he was practiced—he loaded the gun with a few swift movements. A click sounded once the round was inside the rifle.

Both the Captain and Kyle's father stood soaking in the stream. Their eyes jumped to Kyle at the sound of the click, then jumped back to each other. Another spray of water rose between them as they locked hands, pushing back and forth.

"Any sorta help you can provide right now, Malik," the Captain said, "would—be much—"

The father shouted again at his son, "*Shoot him, Kyle!*"

Kyle pointed the rifle the Captain's way. Everything seemed to slow as I stepped to Kyle's side, then in front of the gun.

"Please," I said. "Just please hold on."

CHAPTER FOURTEEN

My hand shook as I rested it on the snout of the gun. The boy looked scared, and I'm sure I did too. Feet splashed in the water behind me as the Captain and Carter struggled to hold their ground.

"This is ugly," I said. "Yeah? And stupid. We don't want to hurt your dad. Believe it or not. We—"

"Don't listen to him, Kyle!" the man said from the water. "Be strong!"

"Look, you've probably seen more awful

things than a kid should've, than anybody should've. And the only way this'll end safe and not be another awful thing is if you hand me that gun. Trust me. Trusting people—it's another way to be strong."

The boy slid his finger off the gun's trigger, then slid it in again.

"But," he said, "*I* enjoy this too," and—*snap*—pulled the trigger back.

CHAPTER FIFTEEN

"I can't believe you socked a kid," the Captain said.

"He tried to *shoot* me," I replied. "If the canteen hadn't stopped the bullet, I would be dead."

"Oh, I was there! Not sayin' you weren't justified. He was a vicious little dude, when you total everything up. But—if his dad hadn't had me in a death grip at the time, I think I woulda fallen over giggling when you socked little Kyle."

"You're the one who decided how to dispatch those hunting dogs."

"Do. Not. Bring up the dogs. That kid made a choice. Those poor dogs didn't have a say in the matter."

I sat next to the Captain, arms around my knees, as our raft drifted creakily downriver. We would float until nightfall, then find a place to sleep, to forage.

We had left the man and his son tied up by the shore. Once I took care of the boy, the Captain and I were able to hold down Carter. The man shouted and spat in the shallow water as we roped his wrists together. As I made my way onto the raft, the old man above us began to blow into his whistle again and again in anger. I watched him get smaller and smaller on his spot on the hillside until I couldn't make out the scowl on his craggy face.

"Yer pretty darn lucky you had that canteen around your neck," the Captain said. The woods around us looked the same as those where we'd left from, but the sun was getting low. "Maybe a luckier person would've gotten this raft moving a little earlier, or wouldn't have got shot down by a family of Kentucky manhunters in the first place. You might have a net total of bad luck, all things considered. But you got pretty lucky with respect to not getting shot."

I rubbed my thumb along the dent left in the heavy canteen. After Kyle had fired the rifle, I'd thought, for a few breaths, that I was gone. And maybe Kyle had thought he got me. Or maybe he stood still from shock—had never shot at anyone from that close before.

I had stumbled back, my ears ringing, my arms spinning in circles. And then I had stopped, patted my chest, and felt no blood, no bullet wound—just dirt and sweat and the stinging hot cavern the round had put in the hunk of metal around my neck. Then, like the Captain said, I socked the kid.

I removed the canteen, looping its strap around one of the raft's bindings, and started to tell the Captain more about earlier. When the boy had pretended to be hurt. How I thought I might've got something through to him.

"Maybe you did. The kid'll probably be thinkin' about today for a while, anyway. Might dawn on him sometime down the road that his dad's nuts," the Captain said. "Oooh— maybe it's *karma* you didn't get plugged, 'specially considering it was the boy's canteen."

"I don't know what that is."

The air filled with cricket chirps and the coos of owls as the night came on, muffling other, faraway sounds. Every so often I'd think I heard horse hooves, never knowing for sure. I pictured Roman the horse clopping on through the woods, keeping pace with our raft.

When it got dark, we figured we were far enough away to start a fire. Even if Carter or Pop-Pop saw the smoke somehow, they had a long enough walk back to their house. The Captain and I nudged the raft toward shore, then both collapsed for a while before looking for tinder.

That night by the flames the Captain went on predicting mutations to come in the family of manhunters. Extra eyes, suction cups on their palms. I began to drift off, half-hearing him, into a heavy sleep overrun by strange and winding dreams.

ABOUT THE AUTHOR

Jonathan Mary-Todd is a dream weaver from the
Twin Cities.

The world is
over.

AFTER THE DUST SETTLED

Can you
survive
what's next?

AFTER THE DUST SETTLED

Fight the Wind

Fix has a gift for machines. If he can fix up an old wind turbine, he and his friends will be able to live at their Iowa camp for as long as they want. Cleo says no way. She'd rather try to find a city that's rumored to be growing in the southwest. But if another rumor is true—that raiders are heading toward the camp—the only real choice will be fight or die.

Pig City

Malik and his friends try to avoid cities, but they look for shelter in downtown Des Moines once a winter storm hits. They're quickly trapped in the middle of a struggle between the city's two biggest gangs: the peaceful members of the Coalition and the forces of Pig City, who want to turn everyone else into hog food.

Plague Riders

When Shep's parents disappeared, he agreed to deliver medicine for the sinister Doctor St. John. The doctor runs the camp of River's Edge with total control, but the pills he makes are the only defense against the nightpox plague. On one trip, Shep learns that his parents may still be alive. With fellow rider Cara by his side, he prepares to escape from River's Edge.

River Run

Freya and her sister have spent years as captives in a Minneapolis basement. After her sister disappears, Freya decides to break out—and finds herself heading down the Mississippi River with a strange young boy. Are the boy's sunny stories about Norlins true? Or will the end of Freya's journey be the most dangerous part?

Shot Down

Malik and the Captain, a gruff inventor, are on a hot air balloon tour of apocalyptic America—until a bullet sends their ride to the ground. A crash landing is just the beginning of their troubles, as the two travelers discover a family that hunts people for sport and begin a run for their lives across the hills and fields of Kentucky.

Snakebite

Beckley's crew has made its way from Montana to South Dakota, living off the land and staying out of trouble. But trouble soon finds them. First, a snake sinks its fangs into the moody Hector. Then a clan of savage kids runs off with Beckley's sister. Will the group's survival knowledge be enough to get her back?

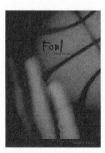

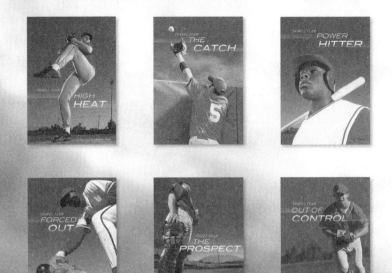

LOOK FOR THESE
TITLES FROM THE

TRAVEL TEAM

COLLECTION.

ARE YOU A SURVIVOR?

SURVIVING SOUTHSIDE

Bad Deal

Beaten

Benito Runs

Plan B

Recruited

Shattered Star

Check out all the books in the collection.